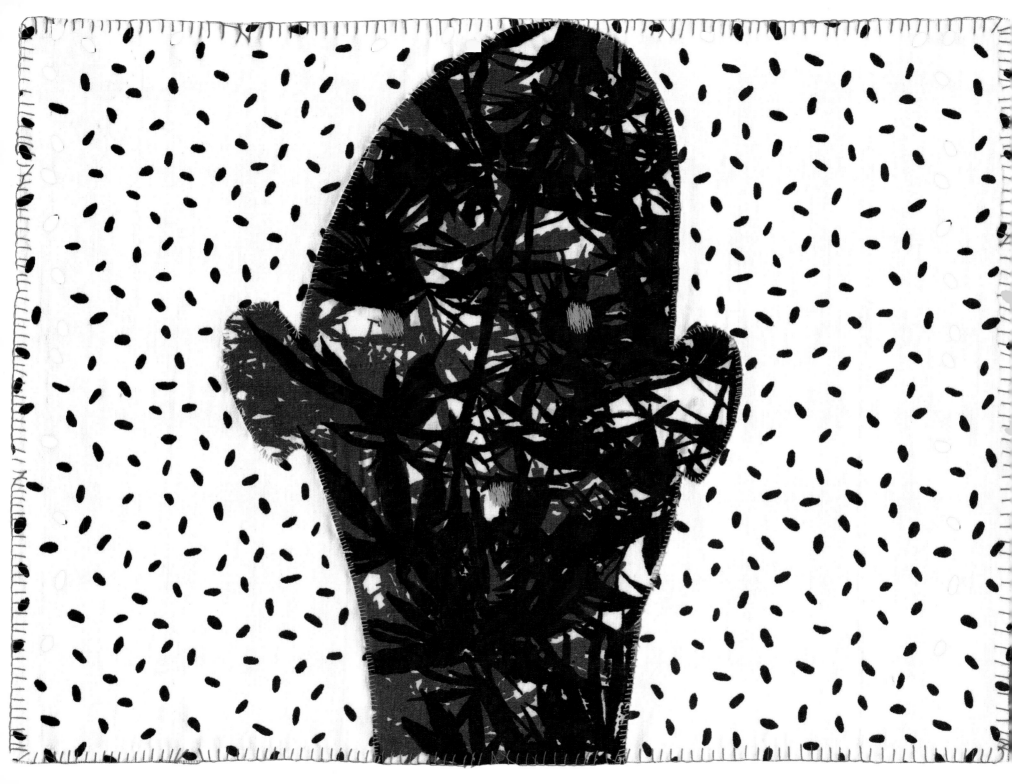

Grannie and the Jumbie

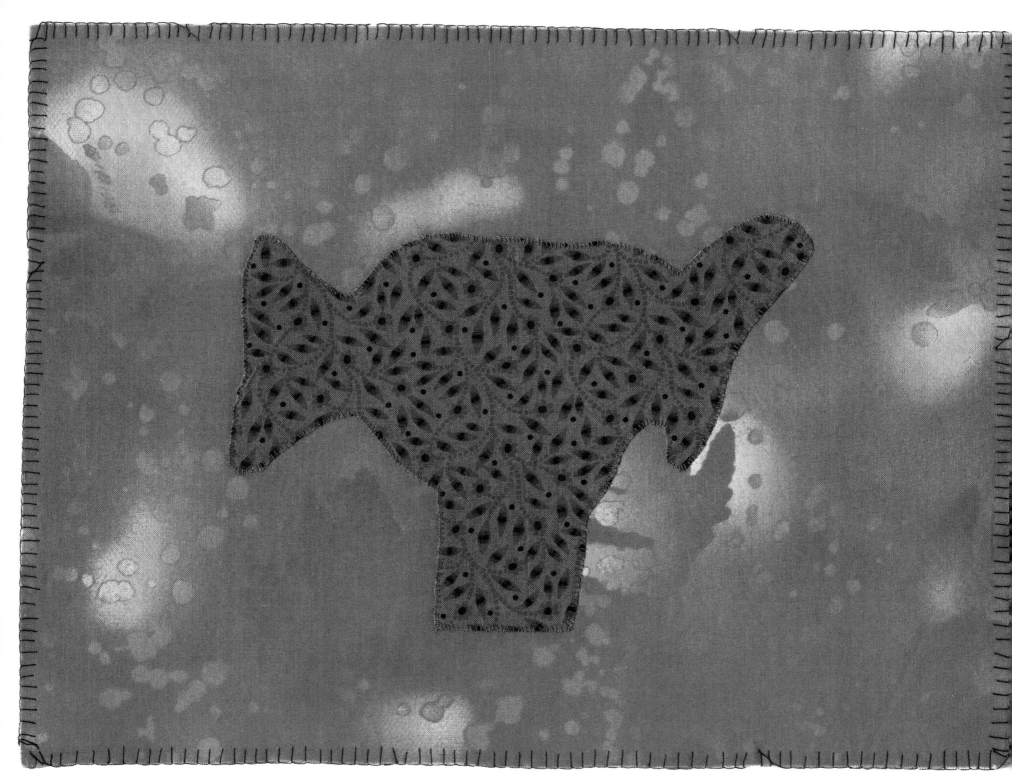

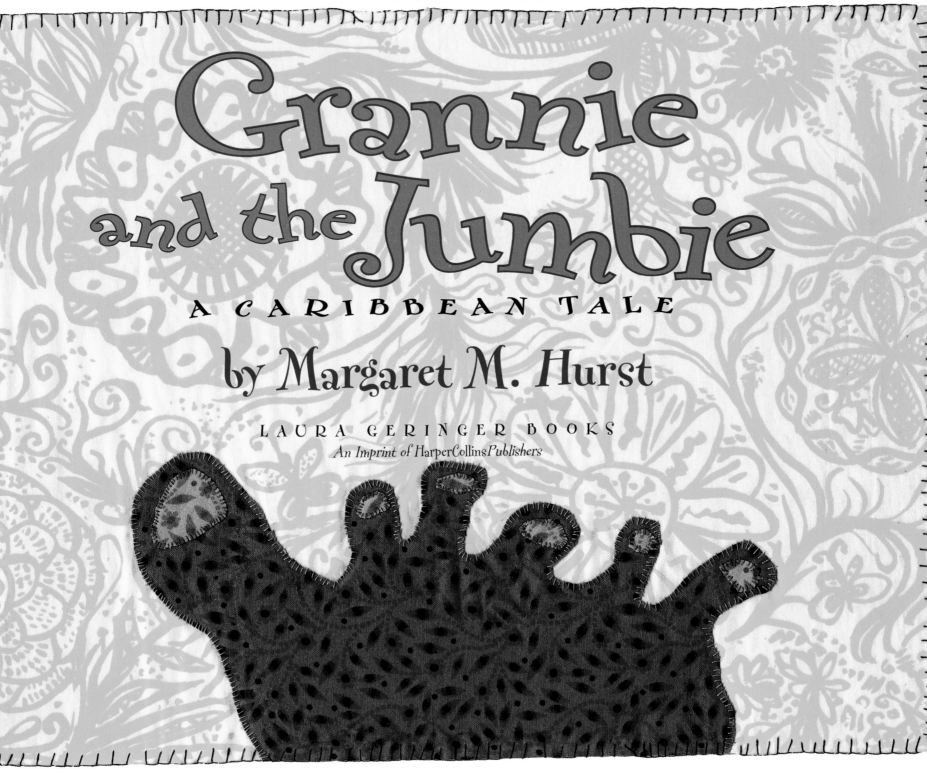

Grannie and the Jumbie

A CARIBBEAN TALE

by Margaret M. Hurst

LAURA GERINGER BOOKS
An Imprint of HarperCollins Publishers

To my teacher David J. Passalacqua,

with love and gratitude.

Thank you for always believing in me.

I would like to thank Ronnie Lawlor, David Passalacqua, Laura Geringer,

Tamar Brazis, Maria Lake, and Alicia Mikles for their great insight and guidance.

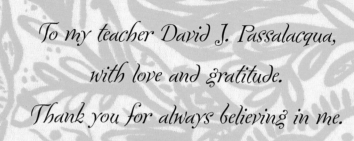

Library of Congress Cataloging-in-Publication Data
Hurst, Margaret M.
   Grannie and the Jumbie / by Margaret M. Hurst
      p.   cm.
   Summary: When a young Caribbean boy does not listen to his grandmother,
an evil spirit threatens to snatch him.
   ISBN 0-06-623632-0 — ISBN 0-06-623633-9 (lib. bdg.)
   [1. Blacks—Caribbean Area—Folklore.   2. Folklore—Caribbean Area.]
I. Title
PZ8.1.H965 Gr   2001
398.2/0972901 E 21   00-054035
                                                                CIP
                                                                 AC

Typography by Alicia Mikles
1 2 3 4 5 6 7 8 9 10
❖
First Edition

ABOUT THE ART

I like to think of all cloth as "story fabric." Some pieces are older and already have a story. Other pieces are new, waiting to create stories.

Most of the fabrics I have used are from St. Thomas. Some of the older pieces are from dresses I remember my mom wearing; some from dresses that she made. Many of the pieces are from the Jim Tillett studios in St. Thomas. On rainy Saturdays my mom would pile friends and cousins into the car and drive us to Mr. Tillett's. He would allow us to silk-screen colorful patterns onto the long rows of white cotton fabric.

The new fabrics I used are now sewn together with the older pieces to create yet another new story, *Grannie and the Jumbie*. I hope this new "fabric story" brings pleasure to everyone who sees and reads it.

Margaret M. Hurst

Emanuel is a very small chile.

He hear about ghost, spirit,
and Jumbie once in a while.

Grannie, she tell him the
spirit story so that he minds:
like keepin' your cap on in the
night ju all the time.

Emanuel, he say one day,
"Why I should be scare dis way?"
He make fun of Grannie:
"Jumbie dis an' Jumbie dat,
an' t'row de salt over you left
shoulder so, to keep away de
spirits, you know!"

Now, Emanuel, he get bold
one day. He play with his shadow
and walk on the cemetery graves!

When he tell his grannie, his grannie say, "Lawd chile, Jumbie come an' take you away!"

Now, Emanuel, he pay his grannie no mind. But that Jumbie had seen him many a time and was angry about Emanuel's boastful ways!

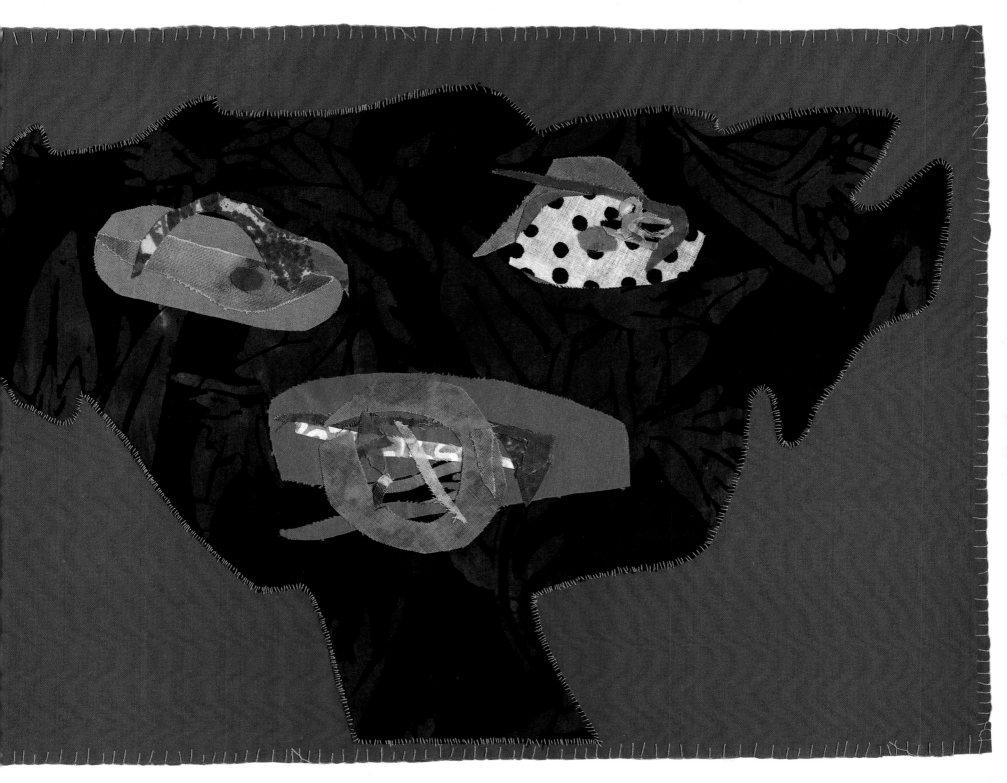

One night Jumbie thinkin' to
himself about Emanuel at home
sleepin' in bed. Jumbie say,
"We see who don' believe in me!"

Well, Jumbie go right on top of Emanuel's bed, ready to take hold of his little head. Suddenly, a big white hand appear over Jumbie's head so near!

And the stern voice of Mista
Mocko Jumbie say, "'Tain' time
fo' de chile to go wit' you—he
have a lot a growin' up to do!"

Mista Mocko Jumbie point
his finger and say, "Now get from
here, you Jumbie you!"

Now, never again would
Emanuel doubt that Jumbie and
spirits lurk about. He listen to
his grannie now.

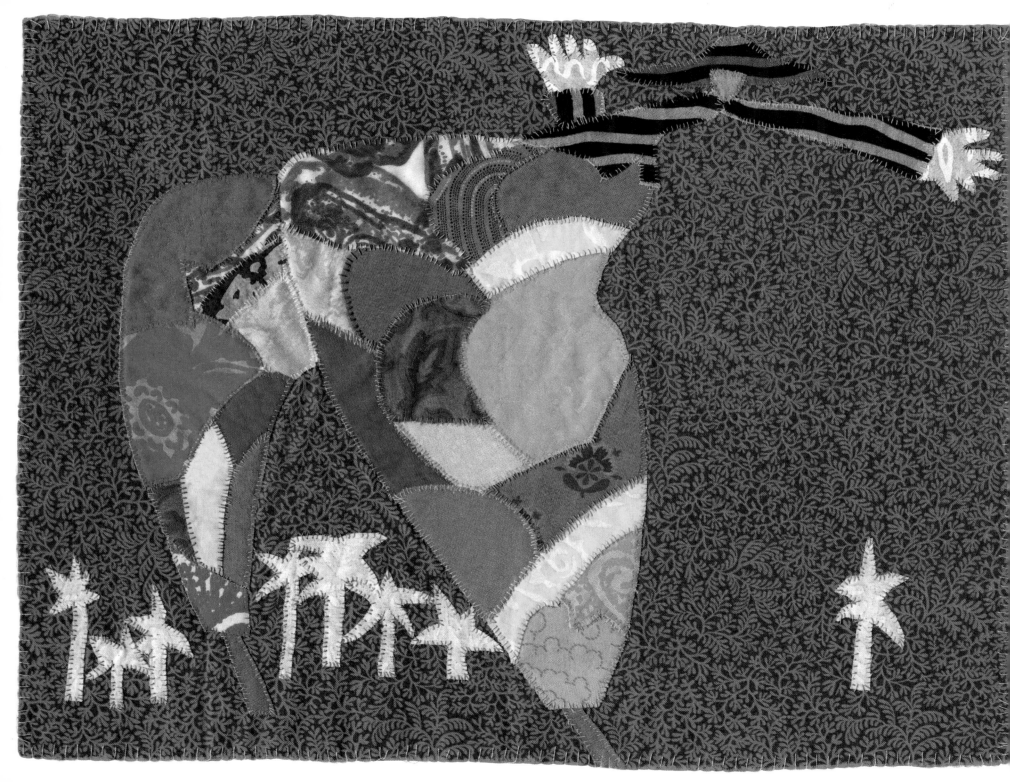

And Mista Mocko Jumbie
say, "Old age and wisdom go
hand in hand."

GLOSSARY

JUMBIE—Of African origin. Ghost, evil spirit, bogeyman.

MOCKO JUMBIE—Of African origin. The spiritual seer and protector of the village. Depending on where you travel and the language spoken, "mocko" means "healer," "seeker," or "protector." One of the main attractions of Carnival on St. Thomas is a stilt walker masquerading as the Mocko Jumbie.

NIGHT JU—night air, vapors that contain Jumbies and other spirits.

WALK ON CEMETERY GRAVES —tempt bad luck.

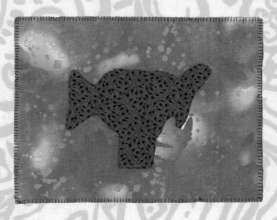

AUTHOR'S NOTE

I have been a red hibiscus, an angelfish, an American colonial woman, a flamingo, a grasshopper, a jellyfish, an Olympic athlete, and a star in the American flag. These magical transformations happened once a year like clockwork in the Carnival parade on St. Thomas.

There were two parades on St. Thomas: the children's parade on Friday, and the adult parade on Saturday. Watching Saturday's parade was the next best thing to being in Friday's. One troupe would be the Garden of Eden, complete with a silky green shimmering snake. Another troupe would enact the life of the pirate Blackbeard, swashbuckling and plundering, while his parrot, Mebucko, sat on his shoulder screeching. Another troupe would be the solar system, bright balls of color, glittering in the noonday sun, bouncing up and down Main Street. It seemed to go on forever, while calypso music, played on steel drums, seemed to carry the throbbing crowds down the street in one dancing rhythm of color.

My best friend, Darcy, and I would watch all this from under the whitewashed arch at the top of the stairs across from the old Western Union cable office. In the cool shade, protected from the sun, we saw everything above the heads of the adults down below. From our high perch we could see the parade and still be far enough away from the clowns. We hated the clowns. They wore white masks with painted eyes, lips, and cheeks. They wore two cones, one on either side of their heads. And worst of all, they cracked long black whips on the street. *Craack, craack!* The sound would send shivers down our backs. Once the clowns passed us by, we relaxed. Suddenly, a huge head would drop down right in front of our faces! We would scream! The face would laugh and disappear, and we'd see the back of the towering Mocko Jumbie dancing down the street, kicking up his red stilts and holding up his skirt so everyone could see his long white pantaloons. From his great height he could see the evil spirits approaching our village and shoo them away. When he disappeared into the crowd, Carnival was over. Until next year!

Margaret M. Hurst